STAGESTRUCK

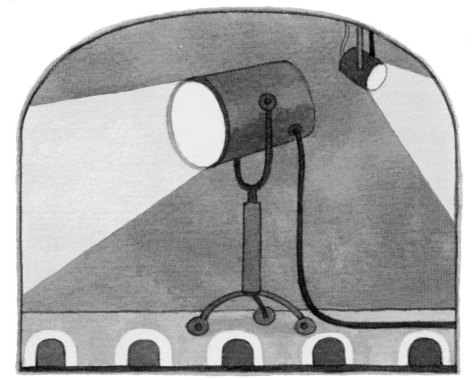

Written and illustrated by

TOMIE DEPAOLA

☆ PUFFIN BOOKS ☆

For "Miss Leah,"
her cousin "Miss Rhoda"—
and "Miss Ranger Diane"
who had her moment in the spotlight, too.

PUFFIN BOOKS
Published by the Penguin Group
Penguin Young Readers Group, 345 Hudson Street, New York, New York 10014, U.S.A.
Penguin Group (Canada), 90 Eglinton Avenue East, Suite 700, Toronto, Ontario, Canada M4P 2Y3
(a division of Pearson Penguin Canada Inc.)
Penguin Books Ltd, 80 Strand, London WC2R 0RL, England
Penguin Ireland, 25 St Stephen's Green, Dublin 2, Ireland (a division of Penguin Books Ltd)
Penguin Group (Australia), 250 Camberwell Road, Camberwell, Victoria 3124, Australia
(a division of Pearson Australia Group Pty Ltd)
Penguin Books India Pvt Ltd, 11 Community Centre, Panchsheel Park, New Delhi - 110 017, India
Penguin Group (NZ), 67 Apollo Drive, Rosedale, North Shore 0745, Auckland, New Zealand
(a division of Pearson New Zealand Ltd)
Penguin Books (South Africa) (Pty) Ltd, 24 Sturdee Avenue, Rosebank, Johannesburg 2196, South Africa

Registered Offices: Penguin Books Ltd, 80 Strand, London WC2R 0RL, England

First published in the United States of America by G. P. Putnam's Sons,
a division of Penguin Putnam Books for Young Readers, 2005
Published by Puffin Books, a division of Penguin Young Readers Group, 2007

10 9 8 7 6 5 4 3 2 1

Copyright © Tomie dePaola, 2005
All rights reserved

THE LIBRARY OF CONGRESS HAS CATALOGED THE G. P. PUTNAM'S SONS EDITION AS FOLLOWS:
dePaola, Tomie.
Stagestruck / written and illustrated by Tomie dePaola.
p. cm.
Summary: Although Tommy fails to get the part of Peter Rabbit in the kindergarten play,
he still finds a way to be the center of attention on stage.
ISBN: 0-399-24338-0 (hc)
[1. Theater—Fiction. 2. Kindergarten—Fiction. 3. Schools—Fiction.]
I. Title.
PZ7.D439Sp 2005 [E]—dc22 2004009261
Designed by Gina DiMassi
Text set in Lomba Medium.
The art was done on Fabriano 140 lb., 100 percent rag handmade paper using acrylics.

Puffin Books ISBN 978-0-14-240899-5

Manufactured in China

Girls and boys," Miss Bird said, "I have some wonderful
news. Our kindergarten class is going to put on the spring
play for the whole school. We are going to do *Peter Rabbit*."

Peter Rabbit! Tommy could hardly sit still. He knew all about *Peter Rabbit.* His mom had read the story to him lots of times.

Tommy whispered loudly to his best friend, Jeannie, "I hope I get to play the part of Peter."

"Tommy," Miss Bird said, "please, no talking."

Tommy tried to pay attention. He really wanted Miss Bird to pick him to play Peter. After all, he had played the Pilgrim John Alden in the Thanksgiving play. He'd remembered all his lines and the teachers had said he was very good.

That wasn't all!

He had been taking tap lessons at Miss Leah's Dancing School since September. Every Saturday morning, he took the beginners' class with four girls and one other boy.

Miss Leah taught them to do Up-Back-Down, Slap-Slap, Up-Back-Down-Down-Down. It was so much fun.

At the end of each lesson, everyone took a bow as if they were onstage. Tommy always looked at Miss Leah, smiled and then bowed just the way Miss Leah had shown them.

"Tommy, you have wonderful stage presence," Miss Leah said. Tommy knew that meant he looked happy to be onstage.

So Tommy was thinking about how Miss Bird would probably ask him to play Peter and how it would feel to be up on the stage with everyone watching him when he heard Miss Bird talking.

"Tommy, I asked you to get out your book. You really must pay attention."

On the way home, Tommy asked Jeannie if she knew who she wanted to be in the play.

"No," Jeannie said. "I could never remember all the words. I'd be too nervous."

"Jeannie, you can be the mouse with peas in her mouth. Peter asks her how to get out of Mr. McGregor's garden. All he hears her say is 'Mumble, mumble, mumble,' because her mouth is full of peas. I'll show you how to do it."

Tommy puffed out his cheeks and mumbled.

Jeannie laughed. "That's really funny, Tommy." Then she puffed out her cheeks and went, "Mumble, mumble, mumble!" "Jeannie, you make a great mouse!" Tommy told her.

The next day, Miss Bird said, "Put your chairs in a circle, everyone. I am going to give out the parts for *Peter Rabbit*."

Tommy whispered loudly to Jeannie, "Now, when Miss Bird asks who would like to play the mouse . . ."

"Tommy, there you go talking again," Miss Bird said.
"Since you cannot pay attention, you will not play Peter
Rabbit. You will be Mopsy!"

"But Mopsy is a girl bunny!" Tommy said.

"Not in our play," Miss Bird told him.

Miss Bird gave the part of Peter Rabbit to Johnny.
Jeannie got to be the mouse.

"At least you get to say 'Mumble, mumble, mumble,'"
Tommy whispered to Jeannie. "The rabbits don't have
any lines at all. We just have to stand there."

That night, before he went to sleep, Tommy remembered something Miss Leah had said in dance class.

"When you are onstage with other people, look at them and react. That means that if they do something funny—laugh. If they are unhappy—look sad. Don't just stand there."

That's what I'll do, Tommy thought. *Whenever Peter does something, Mopsy will react to it!*

Tommy decided to wait until the performance to react. He would surprise everyone.

All during rehearsals, Tommy did exactly what Miss Bird told Mopsy, Flopsy and Cottontail to do.

The day of the play arrived. All the classes filed in and sat
down. The parents of the kindergarten class were there too.
Miss Burke, the principal, came up on the stage.
"Girls and boys, may I present *The Tale of Peter Rabbit*."
Everyone clapped. The play began.

Peter, the bad little bunny, sneaked into Mr. McGregor's garden, where he was not supposed to be.

Mopsy began to react. Mopsy followed Peter with his eyes. Every time Peter did something, Mopsy reacted.

Everyone was laughing at Mopsy.

Jack played Mr. McGregor. He was good and scary.

Jean M. was Mama Rabbit. She was very good too.

Jeannie was perfect as the mouse with peas in her mouth.

Johnny did a nice job as Peter.

But Mopsy stole the show!

Then the play was over. The girls and boys each took a bow and the audience clapped. But when Tommy took his bow, the audience clapped and shouted. Some of the sixth-grade boys even whistled. Someone yelled, "Bravo!"

Tommy was so proud. He looked over at his mom and waved. She waved back.

Miss Mulligan, the fifth-grade teacher, smiled at him and said, "Well, Tommy, you're quite a 'ham.'"

"Thank you, girls and boys," Miss Bird told the class.
"That was very good."

Miss Bird didn't say anything special to Tommy.

Maybe she was sorry that Tommy hadn't played Peter.

Mom was waiting for Tommy when he came outside with Jeannie.

"Jeannie," Mom said, "you were a very good mouse!"

"Tommy showed me how to do it. He should have been Peter," Jeannie said.

On the way home, Mom said, "Well, Tommy, that wasn't very nice of you to steal the show. You were not the star. Peter Rabbit was the star. You were only one of the bunnies. Tomorrow, I want you to tell Johnny you are sorry—and Miss Bird too. Okay?"

Tommy nodded. He started to think that maybe he had made Johnny feel bad. And maybe Miss Bird didn't like him being a "ham," the way Miss Mulligan did.

The next day, Tommy went up to Miss Bird before class and told her he was sorry.

At recess, he told Johnny he was sorry too.

But when Tommy was by himself, he could hear everyone laughing at Mopsy.

He could hear all the clapping when he looked out at the audience and bowed. He could hardly wait to be onstage again.

He was STAGESTRUCK!